What can fireworks do?

Written by Jillian Powell

Illustrated by Laszlo Veres

Collins

What's in this book?

Listen and say

sparklers

Download the audio at www.collins.co.uk/839702

rockets

fireworks

🎧 Jim and Jill are watching the fireworks with Mum and Dad.

Fireworks have got lots of colours.

Mum says, "Look, Jim! Listen, Jill!"

Whizz! Bang!

Jim says, "They're beautiful."

Jill asks, "How many different fireworks are there, Dad?"

Dad says, "There are lots and they can do different things."

These fireworks are rockets. They go up and up!

Whizz!

These are fountain fireworks.
They make lots of beautiful colours.

These fireworks spin and they
make colours.

These fireworks spin, too. They are red and blue and yellow.

Pop!

You can hold sparklers.

Sparklers are very beautiful. You can write your name with them.

This toy car has got a firework in it.
The car runs on the floor.

Whizz!

These fireworks are animal toys. Look!
There is a chicken, a dog, and a snake.

Pop! Whizz!

Some fireworks make smoke.
The smoke is lots of colours.

Crackle! Pop!

Some fireworks make words and numbers. They can ask questions, too.

They can make shapes. Can you see a flower?

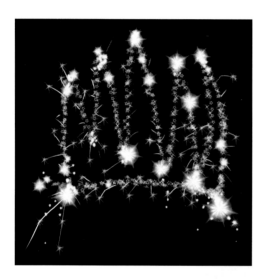

These fireworks are for a celebration.

Many people watch fireworks on television at home.

Animals don't like fireworks.
Bang! Bang!

Don't worry, Pip.

Fireworks are great. But don't stand too near!

What fireworks do you like?
Whizz! Bang! Crackle! Pop!

Picture dictionary

Listen and repeat

fireworks

fountain

rocket

smoke

sparkler

spin

1 Look and match

This toy car has got
a firework in it.

You can write
your name.

They make lots of
beautiful colours.

2 Listen and say

Collins

Published by Collins
An imprint of HarperCollins*Publishers*
Westerhill Road
Bishopbriggs
Glasgow
G64 2QT

HarperCollins *Publishers*
Macken House,
39/40 Mayor Street Upper,
Dublin 1
D01 C9W8
Ireland

William Collins' dream of knowledge for all began with the publication of his first book in 1819.

A self-educated mill worker, he not only enriched millions of lives, but also founded a flourishing publishing house. Today, staying true to this spirit, Collins books are packed with inspiration, innovation and practical expertise. They place you at the centre of a world of possibility and give you exactly what you need to explore it.

© HarperCollins*Publishers* Limited 2020

10 9 8 7 6 5 4 3

ISBN 978-0-00-839702-9

www.collins.co.uk/elt

British Library Cataloguing in Publication Data

A catalogue record for this publication is available from the British Library.

Author: Jillian Powell
Illustrator: Laszlo Veres (Beehive)
Series editor: Rebecca Adlard
Commissioning editor: Zoë Clarke
Publishing manager: Lisa Todd
Product managers: Jennifer Hall and Caroline Green
In-house editor: Alma Puts Keren
Project manager: Emily Hooton
Editor: Barbara MacKay
Proofreaders: Natalie Murray and Michael Lamb
Cover designer: Kevin Robbins
Typesetter: 2Hoots Publishing Services Ltd
Audio produced by id audio, London
Reading guide author: Emma Wilkinson
Production controller: Rachel Weaver
Printed and bound in the UK by Pureprint

MIX
Paper | Supporting responsible forestry
FSC
www.fsc.org
FSC™ C007454

This book is produced from independently certified FSC™ paper to ensure responsible forest management.

For more information visit:
www.harpercollins.co.uk/green

Download the audio for this book and a reading guide for parents and teachers at www.collins.co.uk/839702